If You Were A Writer

If You Were a Writer

Joan Lowery Nixon

illustrated by Bruce Degen

Aladdin Paperbacks

First Aladdin Paperbacks edition 1995
Text copyright © 1988 by Joan Lowery Nixon
Illustrations copyright © 1988 by Bruce Degen

Aladdin Paperbacks
An imprint of Simon & Schuster
Children's Publishing Division
1230 Avenue of the Americas
New York, NY 10020

Also available in a Four Winds Press edition

The text of this book is set in 13-point ITC Bookman Light.
The illustrations are rendered in pen-and-ink and watercolor.

Printed in Hong Kong
10 9 8 7 6 5 4 3 2

The Library of Congress has cataloged the hardcover edition as follows:
Nixon, Joan Lowery. If you were a writer. Summary: Melia tells her writer mother she'd
like to be a writer too, and as the day progresses she receives many helpful suggestions.
[1. Authorship—Fiction] I. Degen, Bruce, ill. II. Title. PZ7.N65Ih 1988 [E] 88-402
ISBN 0-02-768210-2
ISBN 0-689-71900-0 (Aladdin pbk.)

$\mathcal{M}$elia's mother was a writer. Sometimes she sat at her typewriter and her fingers bounced over the keys. Sometimes she stared at the paper in the typewriter and sat so still that Melia thought she was like a fairy-tale princess who had been turned into stone by an evil spell.

"I would like to be a writer, too," Melia told her mother. "Then I could work with a typewriter, the way you do."

Mother shook her head. "A writer doesn't work just with a typewriter. A writer works with words. If you were a writer, you would think of words that make pictures."

Melia stroked the sleeve of her mother's silky blouse, and the words *slippery, slithery,* and *soft* slid into her mind.

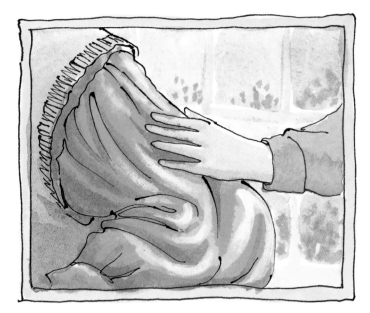

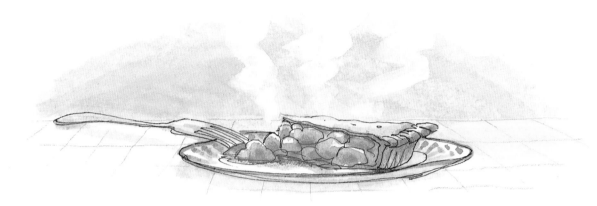

Uncle John, with the whiskery mustache, opened the front door and called, "Where is everybody?"

Melia ran to hug him, and the words *bristly* and *bushy* bounced into her thoughts.

"Grandma asked me to deliver an apple pie," he said. "It's still hot from the oven." He put the pie on the kitchen counter.

Melia took a deep breath. The pie's fragrance turned into the words *spicy, sweet,* and *sour*.

"Don't you want just a taste?" Uncle John whispered. "I think we should sample it!" He cut a narrow wedge and put it on a plate. They each took a bite, and Melia thought of *tangy* and *tart*.

Uncle John went to talk to Melia's mother, who was still staring at the page in her typewriter.

"She's under a spell," Melia told him.

"It's not a bad kind of spell," Mother said. "It's just called 'thinking of what to write next.'"

"When do you get out of the spell?" Melia asked.

"When the right words come," Mother said.

"How do you know what they are?"

"If you were a writer you'd know," Mother said. "You'd feel them inside you, and you'd know they were right."

Melia went outside. She climbed into the branches of the oak tree, and watched afternoon melt into evening, and tried the feel of words.

She saw a flash of gold streak through an orange sunset, and she murmured, "*Glittery* and *glowing.*"

Soon the early evening stars winked through the deep blue sky and the words she whispered were "*Sparkling, silvery, shining,* and *shimmer.*"

And the next day, Melia awoke as the morning exploded into sunlight. She felt warm and cozy as she found the words *bright* and *brilliant* and *blazing*, and knew they were the right ones.

cAt breakfast Melia poured glasses of milk for her little sisters, Nikki and Veronica, and for herself. She took the cereal box away from Nikki, who was still reading the back of it, and dumped some flakes into a bowl.

"Would you like an egg?" Mother asked.

Melia gave the cereal box back to Nikki, who continued to read it. "No, thanks," Melia said. She didn't want to have to think about how to eat eggs. She wanted to think about being a writer instead. "Mom," she asked, "how does a writer tell about what happened in a story?"

Mother took a dirty sock and a tennis shoe from her chair and dropped them on the floor. She sat down and said, "If you were a writer you wouldn't *tell about* what happened in a story. You'd think of words that *show* what is happening. You'd use words that let people see what you see. The characters in your stories wouldn't just walk. They might stomp or stamp."

Nikki looked up and said, "Or stumble or stagger."

"Or tiptoe and trip," Melia suggested.

"Or tumble and twirl," Nikki shouted.

Veronica laughed and bounced in her chair until she spilled her glass of milk.

Mother hurried to find a towel. Melia giggled and said, "And when they were tired they could droop and drop."

"And then what?" Nikki asked.

Melia thought hard until she reached the words that would show what was happening. "Then they could slip between the sheets to snore and sleep!" she said.

cAfter school Melia sat with her mother on the porch swing and watched a large black bee try to squirm inside a quivering honeysuckle blossom.

"Where does a writer get ideas?" Melia asked.

"If you were a writer you would search for ideas," Mother said. "Ideas are everywhere. The more you look for ideas, the more you will find."

"Is the idea the story?"

"No. The idea is just the beginning of the story. If you were a writer you would let ideas bounce in your brain while you watched them grow, and turned them over to see the other sides, and poked them and pushed them and pinched off parts of them, and made them go the way you wanted them to go."

A dog dashed past them, racing down the street. A boy chased the dog, shouting, "Come back! Come back!"

"Maybe the dog and the boy could turn into an idea," Mother said. "Ask yourself, 'What if?'"

"What if what?" Melia wondered.

"What if a diamond necklace has caught on the dog's collar? What if the necklace has been stolen by a pirate? What if the boy is really a detective in disguise? What would happen then?"

Melia thought about the "what ifs."

"I'm going to have a peanut butter and honey sandwich," Mother said. "Would you like one, too?"

Melia followed her mother into the kitchen. Mother poked her head into the kitchen cupboard and said, "That's strange. I just bought a large jar of honey, but I can't find it anywhere."

Melia thought about the missing jar of honey. She asked, "What if we were all in the backyard and a bear squeezed into the house through a front window? What if the bear were under the dining room table, eating the honey, but none of us knew he was there until we sat down at the table for dinner? What would happen then?"

"We'd still need some honey, but we'd have a good idea for a story," Mother answered.

Mother gave Melia half of a peanut butter and strawberry jam sandwich.

Melia took a big bite of the sandwich and asked, with her mouth full, "How do you start a story?"

Mother licked jam from her thumb. "If you were a writer you'd start your stories with something interesting, so people would want to know what happened next."

Melia finished her sandwich, wiped her hands on her jeans, and began looking for Veronica. She found her in the bedroom closet, putting her shoes on the wrong feet.

"I'll tell you a story," Melia said.

"Not now," Veronica said. "I want to go outside and play."

"A little black dog dashed down the street and into an alley," Melia said. "He huddled against the wall and whimpered. A monster from outer space was after him, and the poor little dog didn't know what to do."

"What dog?" Veronica asked. "What monster? Tell me!"

"Later," Melia said. She looked in the den for Nikki. She was lying on her stomach, putting together a jigsaw puzzle.

"Would you like to hear a story about a bear?" she asked.

"No," Nikki said. "I'm busy."

Melia perched on the arm of the sofa. "A hungry bear came out of a forest and across a clearing to a house. He shoved and pushed his way through an open window, and no one who lived in that house knew a dangerous bear was prowling through the kitchen."

Nikki looked up. "A real bear? Whose house? What happened then? Tell me!"

"Later," Melia said, "when I know the rest of the story."

The doorbell rang. Melia ran to answer the door. So did her mother. A delivery man stood there. He held a box in his hands. "Sign here," he said.

Mother signed, took the box, and thanked him before she shut the door. "My books!" she cried. "They're here! The first copies of my new book!"

She sat on the floor in the hallway and tore open the top of the box. She lifted out one of the books and smiled at it and looked through it and hugged it, then handed it to Melia.

Melia liked the picture on the jacket of the book. She liked to see her mother's name on the cover.

"How does an idea turn into a whole story?" she asked.

"If you were a writer, you'd invent an imaginary character who fit into your idea," Mother said.

"Like a boy who helped a little black dog escape from a monster from outer space? Or a girl who saved her family from a bear?" Melia asked.

"Exactly. You'd give this person a problem to solve and maybe friends to help solve it. You'd think of exciting, or funny, or even scary things that would happen to the person in your story.

"If you were a writer, while you ate your cereal, and walked to school, and kicked at leaves, and jumped in puddles, and flopped on the grass, and lay in bed at night waiting for sleep, you would let the story mix and grow with the words in your mind. Together they'd zing and zap and explode into sentences you'd taste and feel and hear. Then you'd know it was time to write down the story so it would never be lost.

"If you were a writer, the stories you wrote might make people laugh, or shiver, or even cry. They'd be your stories. They'd belong to you because they'd be a part of you."

"And I could decide what to do with them," Melia said.

"That's right," Mother said. "You could hug them to yourself like a warm secret, or you could share them with the whole world . . . if you were a writer."

Mother pulled a small pad of paper and a pencil out of her shirt pocket. At the top of the first page she printed A STORY, BY MELIA. She smiled and gave the pad and pencil to Melia. "I think you *are* a writer," she said.

Melia crawled over the box of books to hug her mother. "Oh, yes!" she answered. "I am!"